$\frac{1}{12} = 7$

Let's Have a Play

by Margaret Hillert
Illustrated by Sharon Elzaurdia

DEAR CAREGIVER, The *Beginning-to-Read* series is a carefully written collection of classic readers you may remember from your own childhood. Each book features text comprised of common sight words to provide your child ample practice reading the words that appear most frequently in written text. The many additional details in the pictures enhance the story and offer the opportunity for you to help your child expand oral language and develop comprehension.

Begin by reading the story to your child, followed by letting him or her read familiar words and soon your child will be able to read the story independently. At each step of the way, be sure to praise your reader's efforts to build his or her confidence as an independent reader. Discuss the pictures and encourage your child to make connections between the story and his or her own life. At the end of the story, you will find reading activities and a word list that will help your child practice and strengthen beginning reading skills.

Above all, the most important part of the reading experience is to have fun and enjoy it!

Shannon Cannon

Shannon Cannon,
Literacy Consultant

Norwood House Press • P.O. Box 316598 • Chicago, Illinois 60631
For more information about Norwood House Press please visit our website at
www.norwoodhousepress.com or call 866-565-2900.

LIBRARY OF CONGRESS CATALOGING-IN-PUBLICATION DATA
    Hillert, Margaret.
      Let's have a play / Margaret Hillert ; illustrated by Sharon Elzaurdia. —
    Rev. and expanded library ed.
        p. cm. — (Beginning-to-read series)
      Summary: "On a rainy day, two children decide to make paper-bag puppets and
    put on a play for themselves and their parents"—provided by publisher.
        ISBN-13: 978-1-59953-156-4 (library edition : alk. paper)
        ISBN-10: 1-59953-156-9 (library edition : alk. paper) [1.
    Puppets—Fiction.] I. Elzaurdia, Sharon, ill. II. Title.
    PZ7.H558Led 2008
    [E]—dc22   2007035640

Look at this.
What a day!
What can we do?
What is there for
us to do?

Here is something to play with.
Come here, girl.
What a good girl you are.
We like you.

Now we can look at books.
It is fun to do that.
It is fun to read.

Oh, look here.
Look at this.
Here is something to do.
We can make something.
We can have a play.

Here is how to do it.

See.
Here is how to do it.
Look at this and this.

Get to work.
Work, work, work.
We have to have this
for the play.

Now we have to make
a boy and a girl.
But how do we do that?
Oh, I see.

Father, Father.
Do you have what we want?
Look here.
Here is what we want.

11

Yes, I have something.
Is this it?
Will it work?

We will see.
We will work at it.
We will make something good.

Make something like this.
Make one.
Make two.

Now make one like this.
It will go here.

And make something red.
We have to have this.

And look what comes out.
It is funny.

Oh, oh.
Do not forget something
here and here.

And now make something for up here.

Good. Good.
I have a boy.
You have a girl.

Here is a dog, too.
Look here.
This is a pretty good dog.

And here is something.
Look at this.
Do you like it?
What fun this is!

Oh, this looks good now.
We will have fun with it.
Let's get Mother and Father.
Run, run.

Mother. Father.
Come see what we did.
Oh, it is good.
You will see.
Sit down. Sit down.

Yes, it is good.
You did good work.
We like it.
Now, let's see the play.

READING REINFORCEMENT

The following activities support the findings of the National Reading Panel that determined the most effective components for reading instruction are: Phonemic Awareness, Phonics, Vocabulary, Fluency, and Text Comprehension.

Phonemic Awareness: The long /ā/ sound

Sound Substitution: Say the words on the left to your child. Ask your child to repeat the word, changing the short **a** sound to a long **ā** sound:

back = bake	mad = made	tap = tape	man = main
fat = fate	rack = rake	fad = fade	lack = lake
Sam = same	tack = take	bat = bait	lad = laid
plan = plane	van = vain	salve = save	

Phonics: The long ā spelling

1. Make three columns on a blank sheet of paper and label each with the spellings for long **ā**: a_e, ai, ay

2. Write the following words on separate index cards:

bake	male	pay	day	sail	sale
wave	same	clay	race	nail	wait
say	name	rain	may	face	tail
spray	ray	brain	say	today	aim

3. Ask your child to read each word and place the card under the column heading that represents the long **ā** spelling in the word.

Vocabulary: Theatre Vocabulary

1. Write each of the following words on the upper portion of an index card and read them aloud to your child. Ask your child to repeat the words after you: *play, stage, act.*

2. Explain to your child that sometimes knowing base words can help us figure out new words. In fact, the three words *play*, *stage*, and *act* can help us figure out 10 new words. Add the following words, aligned to the base word and ask your child to make a prediction about their meaning. You may need to provide clues that help your child formulate a prediction:

play	stage	act
playwright	stagehand	actor
playbill	backstage	actress
screenplay	upstage	action
	downstage	

Fluency: Choral Reading

1. Reread the story with your child at least two more times while your child tracks the print by running a finger under the words as they are read. Ask your child to read the words he or she knows with you.

2. Reread the story aloud together. Be careful to read at a rate that your child can keep up with.

3. Repeat choral reading and allow your child to be the lead reader and ask him or her to change from a whisper to a loud voice while you follow along and change your voice.

Text Comprehension: Discussion Time

1. Ask your child to retell the sequence of events in the story.

2. To check comprehension, ask your child the following questions:

   - How do you think the children felt when it was raining?

   - What did the children in the story make? How did they learn to do this?

   - What do you like to do on rainy days?

   - What kind of puppet would you like to make? What would you use to make it?

WORD LIST

Let's Have a Play uses the 64 words listed below. This list can be used to practice reading the words that appear in the text. You may wish to write the words on index cards and use them to help your child build automatic word recognition. Regular practice with these words will enhance your child's fluency in reading connected text.

a	Father	let's	read	up
and	for	like	red	us
are	forget	look(s)	run	
at	fun			want
	funny	make	see	we
books		Mother	sit	what
boy	get		something	will
but	girl	not		with
	go	now	that	work
can	good		the	
come(s)		oh	there	yes
	have	one	this	you
day	here	out	to	
did	how		too	
do		play	two	
dog	I	pretty		
down	is			
	it			

ABOUT THE AUTHOR Margaret Hillert has written over 80 books for children who are just learning to read. Her books have been translated into many different languages and over a million children throughout the world have read her books. She first started writing poetry as a child and has continued to write for children and adults throughout her life. A first grade teacher for 34 years, Margaret is now retired from teaching and lives in Michigan where she likes to write, take walks in the morning, and care for her three cats.

Photograph by Glenna Washburn

ABOUT THE ADVISER Shannon Cannon contributed the activities pages that appear in this book. Shannon serves as a literacy consultant and provides staff development to help improve reading instruction. She is a frequent presenter at educational conferences and workshops. Prior to this she worked as an elementary school teacher and as president of a curriculum publishing company.